This Book Belongs To

. . . .

This edition first published 1999
by Hodder Children's Books

10 9 8 7 6 5 4

A Catalogue record for this book is available from the British Library

ISBN 0340 72669 5

Printed and bound in Great Britain by
Omnia Books Limited, Glasgow

Hodder Children's Books
A Division of Hodder Headline Limited
338 Euston Road
London NW1 3BH

TJ's Sunflower Race

Rose Impey

Anna Currey

Hodder Children's Books

a division of Hodder Headline Limited

For Jan and Jan

Chapter One

Abi was round at TJ's house.
They were in the garden with
nothing to do.
"I'm bored," said Abi.
TJ was bored too, which made
her bad-tempered.

TJ's little sister, Josie, came out and waved her toy rabbit in TJ's face.

"Don't do that," said TJ. "Go away."

So Josie waved Pinky through a hole in the fence instead.

Next door Mrs Bee was planting seeds. She had a few left over. "Hi, Josie," she said. "Would you and Pinky like these?"

"She'll only eat them," said TJ.
"She eats everything."
"Well, sunflower seeds won't hurt her," said Mrs Bee.
"My hamster eats those," said Abi.

Josie set off with the packet to show her mum.

"Sunflowers grow ever so big," said Mrs Bee.
"How big?" asked Abi.
"As high as a house - if you're lucky."

"We could have a race!" said TJ.
"Yes!" shouted Abi. "First one to reach the roof wins!"

The girls ran down the garden to catch up with Josie.
TJ grabbed the seed packet.
"Mine! Mine!" yelled Josie.

TJ tipped the seeds into her hand.
There were just five.

"Two each and one left over," said Abi.
TJ put the smallest seed in the packet and gave it back to Josie.
She stopped crying and wandered off.

TJ told Abi to close her eyes.
She put two seeds in each hand.
Then she made two fists and held them out in front of her.
"Left or right?" she said.
"Right," said Abi.

And that was how the race started.

Chapter Two

TJ and Abi planted their seeds
in big flowerpots.
They stuck their names in them.

Then they watered them and waited for them to grow.

After Abi went home, TJ started to feel bad about taking Josie's seeds.
She tried to help Josie plant her seed too.

But when she looked inside the seed packet it was empty.
"I knew you'd eat it," said TJ.

But Josie hadn't eaten it. She'd hidden it in her secret place.

Josie had a small hole she could crawl into, behind the roses. No one else knew about it, only Scruffy their dog.
And Scruffy wasn't telling anyone.

Two weeks later, the first green
seedling poked through.
It was one of Abi's seeds.
"I win! I win!" she shouted.

"We've only just started," said TJ.

By the end of the week all four seedlings were through.
And now the race was really on.

In the cool, dark soil
Josie's secret sunflower
began to push through.

No one knew about this one,
only Josie and Pinky.
And Pinky wasn't
telling anyone.

Chapter Three

When the school holidays came,
the heatwave started.
There was no rain.

TJ and Abi had to water their plants every day.
Abi brought a little bottle of plant food from home and poured a few dark drops into the watering can.

"What's that?" asked TJ.
"Just something to make them grow," said Abi, mysteriously.
"That's not fair," said TJ.
"There's no rule against it," said Abi.
It was a race after all.

Sometimes Josie
forgot to water
her plant,
if she was too
busy making
a tent for Scruffy,

or giving Annie Macavity
a ride round
the garden,

or dressing up
as a flower fairy.

But Josie's sunflower still got watered, because every time Mum washed up she poured the washing-up water over the roses.

And over Josie's secret sunflower, too.

Every day TJ and Abi measured
their plants.
Soon they were past the end
of the ruler.
They grew so tall they started
to lean over. So TJ and Abi found
sticks to tie them to.

Then all four plants got greenfly. TJ and Abi spent the whole afternoon looking for ladybirds to eat the greenfly. But as fast as they found them the ladybirds flew away.
"You stand guard while I find some more," said Abi.

"I've got my eye on you," TJ told the ladybirds.

Josie's plant didn't need tying up because it had the roses to support it.

Now the roses knew the secret too. But the roses weren't telling anyone.

Chapter Four

By the middle of August it was so hot that TJ and Abi had to water their plants twice a day.

"This is a full-time job," said TJ.
"Next week, when I'm in Spain," said Abi, "you'll have to water mine as well."

"That's not fair," said TJ.
"If you don't, they'll die," said Abi, "and that's not fair, either."
Abi made TJ promise.
"Cross my heart and hope to die," she said crossly.

While Abi was on holiday,
TJ's friend Danny came round
and helped TJ measure her
sunflowers.

"I'll never win at this rate,"
she said. "I wish there was
something else I could do to
make them grow."

"You could talk to them," said Danny.
"Talk to them?" TJ looked surprised.
"My granddad talks to his beans all the time."
"Does it work?" said TJ.
"Does it!" said Danny. "They're gigantic."

TJ felt a bit shy at first,
but she soon got used to it.
She even gave them names.

"Well done," she whispered.
"You've grown ten centimetres this week. You're the best sunflowers in the whole wide world."

TJ didn't talk to Abi's sunflowers; she hadn't promised to do that. But when Abi's postcard arrived TJ took it out and read it to them.

"Abi says, 'It's even hotter in Torromelinos. I'm learning to dive in the hotel swimming pool. See you soon.
P.S. Don't forget to water my plants!!!' "
"As if I would," said TJ.

Each afternoon, when it got too hot, Josie took Pinky into her secret place and read him a story. Her sunflower must have liked the stories too. It grew even taller, way up into the roses. Now Josie could hardly see it either.

It was still a secret sunflower, and Josie wasn't telling anyone.

Chapter Five

When Abi came home from Spain
she brought a pair of sunglasses
for TJ and some shells
to put round her sunflowers.
"Wow! They've
grown so much
while I was
away," she said.
"That's because I
watered them every
day," said TJ.

By the end of August, all four sunflowers were nearly reaching TJ's bedroom windowsill.

TJ could kneel on her bed and touch them.

Abi's was the first to get there. "Look! Look! I've won!" she shouted.

"No you haven't," said TJ. "It's got to reach the roof."

After that, Abi's sunflowers seemed to stop and wait for TJ's to catch up. Then all four stopped growing. They just hung their heads.

The flowers still hadn't opened.
"What's going to happen now?"
said TJ crossly.
"I don't know," said Abi. She was
cross, too.

But Josie's sunflower
was still growing.
Round the corner,
behind the roses,
it was stretching
up towards the
roof.
Quietly,
secretly.

It wasn't quite ready to come out.
Not just yet.

TJ and Abi had been back at school for more than a week, when the first sunflower opened and showed its yellow face to the sun.

"Now I've really, really won!"
shrieked Abi.
"It has to reach the roof,"
TJ told her again. "That was
the rule."
"What if none of them does?"
said Abi. "Then what?"

"I don't know," said TJ.

In another week all the flowers
were open.
Four big yellow heads nodded
outside TJ's bedroom window.

"Don't they look a picture," said Mrs Bee.
"Lovely," said Mum.
"But nobody's *won*," said TJ, "there's got to be a winner."
"You're both winners," said Mum.

But TJ and Abi wanted a proper winner.
"Never mind," said Mrs Bee.
"I'll take a photo of them."

TJ and Abi ran upstairs
and knelt on TJ's bed
and waved to Mrs Bee.

Mrs Bee had to go right to
the end of the garden to get
a good picture.

Suddenly, out of the corner of her eye, she spotted another yellow face winking at her from among the roses.

"I think there is a winner, after all," she called. "Come and look."

Peeping round the side of the house, Josie's secret sunflower nudged the corner of the roof and smiled shyly for the camera.

And Josie smiled, too.